What Is Light?

SIMON & SCHUSTER BOOKS FOR YOUNG READERS

An imprint of Simon & Schuster Children's Publishing Division

1230 Avenue of the Americas, New York, New York 10020

Text copyright © 2018 by Markette Sheppard

Illustrations copyright © 2018 by Cathy Ann Johnson

Previously published in 2018 by Bolden Books, an imprint of Agate Publishing

SIMON & SCHUSTER BOOKS FOR YOUNG READERS is a trademark of Simon & Schuster, Inc.

For information about special discounts for bulk purchases, please contact Simon & Schuster
Special Sales at 1-866-506-1949 or business@simonandschuster.com.

The Simon & Schuster Speakers Bureau can bring authors to your live event. For more
information or to book an event, contact the Simon & Schuster Speakers Bureau
at 1-866-248-3049 or visit our website at www.simonspeakers.com.

Book design by Morgan Krehbiel

The text for this book was set in ArcherPro.

The illustrations for this book were rendered digitally.

Manufactured in China

0122 SCP

First Simon & Schuster Books for Young Readers hardcover edition May 2020

10 9 8 7 6 5 4 3

Library of Congress Cataloging-in-Publication Data

Names: Sheppard, Markette, author. | Johnson, Cathy Ann, 1964– illustrator.

Title: What is light? / Markette Sheppard ; illustrated by Cathy Ann Johnson.

Description: New York : Simon & Schuster Books for Young Readers, [2020] | Audience: Ages
4-8. | Audience: Grades K-1. | Summary: Illustrations and easy-to-read, rhyming text introduce
children to the many sources of light in the world, from the sun to the smile on a friend's face.

Identifiers: LCCN 2019050885 (print) | LCCN 2019050886 (ebook) | ISBN 9781534476516
(hardcover) | ISBN 9781534476523 (ebook)

Subjects: CYAC: Stories in rhyme. | Light—Fiction. | Friendship—Fiction. | African Americans—
Fiction.

Classification: LCC PZ8.3.S55112 Wh 2020 (print) | LCC PZ8.3.S55112 (ebook) | DDC [E]—dc23

LC record available at https://lccn.loc.gov/2019050885

LC ebook record available at https://lccn.loc.gov/2019050886

What Is Light?

BY Markette Sheppard

ILLUSTRATED BY Cathy Ann Johnson

A DENENE MILLNER BOOK

SIMON & SCHUSTER BOOKS FOR YOUNG READERS
NEW YORK LONDON TORONTO SYDNEY NEW DELHI

Light can be many things,

such as the brightness our sun brings.

The twinkle of a faraway star . . .

The buzzing of a firefly

captured in a jar . . .

And then that feeling
when you let it go . . .

That spark in your eyes
is like a glow.

A bright green leaf

floating in the wind . . .

The smile on your face

when you see a friend.

Oh, light can be so many things!

A mother's love · · ·

A turtledove . . .

A colorful butterfly

flapping its wings . . .

What is the light that can
be seen around you?

It can be found in everything that you do.

And especially

inside of
you!